Some Cannot Fly

Written by Jo Windsor

Look at this bird.
This bird cannot fly.

emu

Look at this bird.
This bird cannot fly.

cassowary

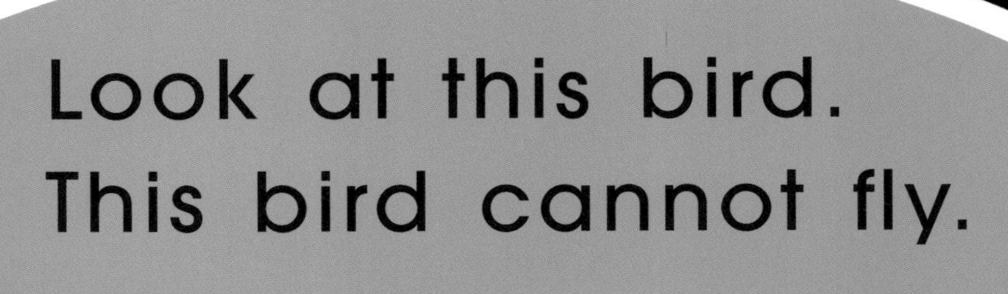

Look at this bird.
This bird cannot fly.

kakapo

Look at this bird.
This bird cannot fly.

kiwi

Look at this bird.
This bird cannot fly.

ostrich

Look at this bird.
This bird can swim.

penguin

Index

birds that
cannot fly . . . 2-11

birds that
can swim . . 12-13

Guide Notes

Title: Some Birds Cannot Fly
Stage: Emergent – Magenta
Genre: Nonfiction (Expository)
Approach: Guided Reading
Processes: Thinking Critically, Exploring Language, Processing Information
Written and Visual Focus: Photographs (static images), Index, Labels
Word: 48

FORMING THE FOUNDATION

Tell the children that this book is about birds that cannot fly.
Talk to them about what is on the front cover. Read the title and the author.
Focus the children's attention on the index and talk about the different categories to be found in the book.
"Walk" through the book, focusing on the photographs and talk about the different animals and where they are.

Read the text together.

THINKING CRITICALLY

(sample questions)

After the reading

- How do you think these birds can get away from danger?
- Why do you think some birds cannot fly?

EXPLORING LANGUAGE

(ideas for selection)

Terminology
Title, cover, author, photographs

Vocabulary
Interest words: bird, fly, swim
High-frequency words: look, at, this